BITTER HERBS

A Short Chronicle

MARGA MINCO

Translated by Jeannette K. Ringold

EBURY
PRESS

1 3 5 7 9 10 8 6 4 2

Ebury Press, an imprint of Ebury Publishing
20 Vauxhall Bridge Road,
London SW1V 2SA

Ebury Press is part of the Penguin Random House group of companies
whose addresses can be found at global.penguinrandomhouse.com

Penguin
Random House
UK

The publisher gratefully acknowledges the support of the
Dutch Foundation for Literature

N ederlands
letterenfonds
dutch foundation
for literature

Text copyright © Marga Minco 1957
English translation copyright © Jeannette K. Ringold 2020

The rights of Marga Minco and Jeannette K. Ringold to be identified as
the author and translator of this work, respectively, have been asserted in
accordance with the Copyright, Designs and Patents Act 1988

First published by Ebury Press in 2020
Originally published with the title *Het bittere kruid* in the Netherlands in 1957 by
Uitgeverij Bert Bakker/Daamen (now Uitgeverij Prometheus), Amsterdam

www.penguin.co.uk

A CIP catalogue record for this book is available from the British Library

ISBN 9781529106497

Typeset in 12.5/14.75 pt Garamond MT Std
by Integra Software Services Pvt. Ltd, Pondicherry

Printed and bound in Great Britain by Clays Ltd, Elcograf S.p.A.

MIX
Paper from
responsible sources
FSC
www.fsc.org   FSC® C018179

Penguin Random House is committed to a sustainable
future for our business, our readers and our planet. This
book is made from Forest Stewardship Council® certified
paper.

Through my head rolls a train
full of Jews. I click on the past
as if it were a railroad switch . . .

Bert Voeten, *The Train*

In memory of my parents
Dave and Lotte
Bettie and Hans

Contents

One day

It started one day when my father said, 'Let's go and see if everyone is back.' We'd been away for a few days. All of Breda had been ordered to evacuate. We had hurriedly packed a suitcase and joined the endless lines of people leaving the city in the direction of the Belgian border. Bettie and Dave were living in Amsterdam at the time. 'They won't be affected by any of this,' my mother said.

It was a long, dangerous journey. We carried the suitcase on a bicycle. Overstuffed bags were hanging from the handlebars. Bomb fragments and machine-gun bullets flew over our heads. Now and then someone was hit; then a small group would stay behind. Close to the Belgian border we found shelter with farmers. After two days we saw German troops driving down the country road and several hours later the evacuees returned to the city.

'The danger has passed,' a fellow townsman announced. So we went back with him.

At home, everything was as we had left it. The table was still set. Only the clock had stopped. My mother immediately threw open the windows. Across the street a woman hung her blankets over the balcony. Elsewhere someone shook out rugs as if nothing had happened.

I went into the street with my father. Our next-door neighbour, who was standing in his front garden, came to the gate when he saw us walking toward him.

'Have you seen them yet?' he asked. 'They're pretty impressive, aren't they?'

'No,' said my father, 'I haven't seen anything yet. We're going to have a look.'

'The whole city is crawling with them,' said the neighbour.

'I'm not surprised,' said my father. 'Breda is a garrison town, so you can expect that sort of thing.'

'I wonder how long they'll stay,' the neighbour said.

'Not long, I assure you,' declared my father.

'What about you?' asked the neighbour. He inched closer. 'What will your family do now?'

'We?' said my father. 'We aren't going to do anything. Why should we?'

The neighbour shrugged and plucked a leaf out of his hedge. 'When you hear what they do over there . . .'

'Things won't get that bad here,' said my father.

We walked on. At the end of the street we ran into Mr Van Dam.

'Well, well,' he said, 'we're all back.'

'So it seems,' said my father. 'Everyone's back home, safe and sound. Have you spoken to many of the others yet?'

'I sure have,' said Mr Van Dam, 'several. The son of the Meier family has apparently gone all the way to the French border with some friends.'

'Oh well,' said my father, 'boys like that are always looking for adventure. Can't say I blame them.'

'Your other daughter and your son didn't go with you?'

'No,' said my father, 'they're in Amsterdam. They'll be fine there.'

'For the time being at any rate,' said Mr Van Dam.

'Well, we're off,' my father said.

'What did Mr Van Dam mean by "for the time being"?' I asked as we kept walking.

'He's pessimistic, I think.'

'Just like our next-door neighbour,' I said.

My father frowned. 'It's hard to say what's going to happen,' he said. 'We'll just have to wait and see.'

'Do you think they'll do the same to us as they did to . . .' I didn't finish my sentence. I thought about all the gruesome stories that I'd heard during the past few years. It had always seemed so far away.

'Nothing like that can ever happen here,' said my father. 'Things are different here.'

A thick cloud of tobacco smoke hung in the small office of Mr Haas's clothing shop on Catharinastraat. Several members of the congregation had gathered, as if for a meeting. Short, stocky Mr Van Buren swivelled around in his office chair, gesticulating wildly. He had a rasping voice. When we went in, he was talking about holding a special service.

'It sounds like a good plan,' my father said.

'Will all that praying do any good?' asked Mr Haas's son. Apparently, no one had heard him, as his remark was ignored. I was sorry I'd come here with my father, for I realised it would be a while before he could get away. Since I didn't feel like sitting in that smoky room, I went through the hall to the shop. No one was there. I walked past the counters and shelves filled with clothes. As a child I had often played there with Mr Haas's children. We used to hide behind the coats and the boxes, adorn ourselves with the ribbons and remnants from the workshop, and play shop after business hours. The same smell still hung in the air, sweetish and dry, the way new textile smells. I wandered through the narrow halls to the workshop and the stockroom. It felt like a Sunday. No one would come and buy anything today or be measured for a new coat. I sat down on a stack of boxes in a corner of the workshop and waited. The room was rather dark because the shutters were closed and the only light was coming from the hall. A coat, with the tacking thread still in it, was hanging against the wall. Perhaps no one would ever pick it up now. I took it off the hanger, put it on, and looked at myself in the mirror. It was much too long.

'What on earth are you doing?' It was my father's voice. I was startled because I hadn't heard him approach.

'Trying on a coat,' I said.

'This is no time to be thinking of a new coat.'

'I don't want this one anyway,' I said.

'I've looked everywhere for you. Are you coming?'

I took off the coat and hung it back up. After sitting in the dark so long, the bright sunlight made me squint. The streets were busy. Many unfamiliar cars and motorcycles drove past us. A soldier asked somebody in front of us how to get to the market square. It was explained to him with much waving of hands and arms. The soldier clicked his heels, saluted, and set off in the direction that he'd been shown. German soldiers were now passing us constantly. We calmly walked past them.

'You see,' said my father when we were almost home, 'they aren't doing anything to us.' As we passed the neighbour's gate, he muttered again, 'They aren't doing anything to us.'

Kloosterlaan

When my sister and I were little, the other children used to call us names as we were leaving school. They'd frequently be lying in wait for us at the end of Kloosterlaan. 'Come along,' Bettie would say firmly as she grabbed my hand. Sometimes I'd meekly suggest taking another street or turning around, but she kept walking, pulling me along, straight toward the jeering gang. Lashing out right and left with her schoolbag, my sister forced her way through the pack of children who punched and pushed us from all sides. I wondered why we were different.

'My teacher says Jews are bad,' a neighbour's child who went to a Catholic school once told me. 'You killed Jesus.'

At the time I didn't even know who Jesus was. I once saw my brother fight a boy who wouldn't stop calling him a 'kike'. The kid only shut up when Dave knocked him down. When Dave came home with a bleeding head, my father showed us a scar on his temple that he'd got during his school years when a kid had scratched him with a nail. 'In Twente where I grew up, they also used to call us names,' he said.

I had a friend who used to pick me up on our way to school. Her name was Nellie and she was light blonde. She always remained standing on the doorstep but never came in. If the door was open, she would peer into the hall with curiosity. 'What's it like in your house?' she asked one day.

'Come in and take a look,' I said.

But she didn't dare because her mother had forbidden her to enter a Jewish house. I was eleven then, old enough to be able to laugh it off. I told her that my father used to eat a soup made out of little children, which my mother had cooked for him. After that my friend would come in secretly, without her mother's knowledge.

When we were older, we hardly noticed things like that any more. Children under ten are often crueller than adults. I remember that we had a maid who had to ask her priest's permission to work for us. The priest gave his consent and even told her she didn't have to eat fish on Friday, which was lucky for her because on Friday evenings we used to have elaborate dinners with all sorts of meat dishes.

My father was a religious man who liked having a home in which Jewish law and ritual practices were maintained. It must have been painful for him to see his children gradually abandon these customs in their eagerness to participate in everything and hang around with their non-Jewish friends. Dave, as the oldest, had the hardest time, since he was the first to break with tradition. He made it easy for us, his sisters. I still remember the first time I ate a rabbit leg with a friend in an automat. I was doing something that was strictly forbidden. I hesitated for a moment before biting into it, the way you do before jumping into a swimming pool at the beginning of the season. But if you don't give up, it bothers you less the second time. During the occupation, the word 'forbidden' took on another significance for us. Jews were forbidden to go to cafés and restaurants, theatres and cinemas, swimming pools and parks. Owning a bicycle, a telephone, or a radio was also forbidden. So much was forbidden.

If I'd still been a little girl, I would definitely have wondered if it really was because we had killed Jesus.

During the first year of the war, I fell ill. I had to spend a long time in a convalescent hospital while my parents moved to the city of Amersfoort to live with my brother, who had married in the meantime.

I was in the pavilion of a hospital in Utrecht and was forbidden to get out of bed. For me, the state of war had been replaced by the state of my sedimentation rate. The distinction that the doctors and nurses made with regard to us patients was between serious and less serious cases of TB. Perhaps that was why I didn't mind my long convalescence as much as I would have during normal times. Only during visiting hours did the war and the latest regulations enter my sickroom. But it was as if it didn't involve me, as if it were taking place in another world.

Once I started getting better, I could no longer avoid it. I knew that once I left the hospital I would be stepping right back into Kloosterlaan, that the gang of jeering children would be waiting for me, and that I'd have to go through it all again.

The stars

The stars

From the window of my room I saw my father approaching in the distance. I'd left the hospital a few weeks earlier. I was supposed to rest several hours a day, but had made a complete recovery.

So far all I knew of Amersfoort was this street. It was in a quiet suburb with new duplexes surrounded by gardens.

My father was walking with short, brisk steps. He doffed his hat with a flourish to a woman picking flowers in her front garden. She apparently said something to him, for he slowed his steps for a moment. When he reached our house, I saw that he was holding a package. A small brown package.

I went downstairs, stuck my head around the living room door and announced, 'Father's coming with a package.'

'What's in it?' I asked at the front door.

'In what?' asked my father, calmly hanging up his coat and hat after placing the package on the coat rack.

'Oh, honestly!' I said impatiently. 'In the package that you just put down.'

'You'll see,' he said. 'Come.'

I followed him in. He set the package on the table while everyone looked on with curiosity. It had been wrapped with string and he patiently untied the knots, then opened the paper. It was the yellow stars.

'I brought some for all of us,' he said, 'so you can sew them on all your coats.'

My mother took one out of the package and examined it closely. 'Let me go and see if I have some yellow thread on hand,' she said.

'It's orange,' I said, 'you ought to use orange thread for it.'

'If you ask me,' said my brother's wife, Lotte, 'it would be better to use thread in the colour of your coat.'

'It'll look awful on my red jacket,' said Bettie, who had come over from Amsterdam to stay with us for a couple of days.

'I'll leave it to you to figure out how to do it,' said my father. 'As long as you remember that they should be chest-high on the left side.'

'How do you know that?' asked my mother.

'It was in the paper,' said my father. 'Didn't you read it? They have to be clearly visible.'

'Goodness, you've brought a lot of them,' said my mother, handing out a few stars to each of us. 'Could you get that many?'

'Oh yes,' said my father, 'as many as I wanted.'

'That's convenient,' she said. 'Now we can save some for our summer clothes.'

We took the coats from the coat rack and started sewing on the stars. Bettie worked very carefully with small, invisible stitches. 'You have to hem them,' she said to me when she saw me sewing one on my coat with big messy stitches. 'It'll look much neater.'

'That star shape is really awkward,' I said. 'How can you get a hem in these wretched points?'

'You have to tack the hem first,' said Bettie. 'Next you pin it to your coat, sew it on and take out the tacking thread. That's guaranteed to make it look good.'

I tried again, but I wasn't as clever with a needle and thread as my sister. My star wound up being lopsided.

'Now you can't read what it says,' I said, sighing. 'But that won't be a problem. They'll know anyway.'

'Look at this,' said Lotte. 'It fits right into the check pattern of my coat.' We looked at her coat, which she instantly put on.

'Very nice,' said my mother, 'you've sewed it on very neatly.'

Then Bettie slipped on her coat as well and the two of them paraded through the room.

'Just like on the Queen's Birthday,' I said. 'Wait a minute, I'll put mine on too.'

'That star is bound to fall right off,' said Lotte.

'Oh no,' I said, 'it'll never come off.'

'What on earth are you doing?' asked Dave. He was standing in the doorway, staring at us in amazement.

'We're sewing on the stars,' said Lotte.

'I'm looking for my coat,' he said. 'Has anyone seen my coat?'

'It's right here,' Lotte said. 'I haven't got around to it yet.'

'I have to pop out,' said Dave. 'Can I still wear it without a star?'

'It's still OK today,' my father said.

'Shall I sew it on for you?' I offered. 'I'm very good at it.'

'No, let me still be a normal human being today,' said Dave.

He opened the garden gate and walked down the street, while the five of us watched him as if there were something very special about him.

The bottle

My brother looked closely at the small medicine bottle he was holding. It was filled with a brownish liquid.

'Are you ill?' I asked.

'No,' he said, 'why?'

'Isn't that medicine?'

'It's for tomorrow,' he said.

'For ... er ... nerves?' I asked.

'No, for something else,' he said.

'Is it dangerous?' asked Lotte.

'Maybe,' he said. He pulled out the cork and sniffed it.

'So should you be taking it?' she said.

'Who knows?' said Dave. He put the bottle in his pocket and walked into the garden through the open French doors. He picked up a pebble from the gravel path and flung it over the gate. I had followed him out to sit under the awning in my deckchair because I still wasn't allowed to expose my skin completely to the sun. Only my legs. I moved the chair so that the sun would only hit my feet.

'It's certainly taken a long time, hasn't it?' I said to Dave, who was staring into the garden with his back to me.

'What took a long time?' he asked.

'My illness,' I said. 'I'm tired of being a convalescent.'

'Be glad that you're better,' he said.

'Will it make you sick?' I asked.

'What will?'

'The . . . bottle,' I said hesitantly.

He shrugged. 'It makes you feel miserable,' he said, 'which is what it's supposed to do.' He turned and went back inside. The next day my father and he, along with all the Jewish men in Amersfoort, were required to undergo a physical examination to see if they were fit for the work camps. My father didn't think he'd pass the exam. To his delight, he'd developed a rash. 'They won't want me,' he said. 'You'll see.' I suspected that he was doing something to make it worse. I knew that Dave was also intent on trying to find a way to avoid ending up in a work camp. As soon as he heard the news, he called on a number of his acquaintances and, after a few days, he claimed to have found a solution. At first I didn't know what the medicine bottle had to do with it. After all, I had always associated medicine with getting better.

Violin music floated out from the living room. I hadn't heard my brother play in a long time. I turned around in my chair and peered inside. Dave was standing in the middle of the room, improvising a czardas, while Lotte watched. His head was tilted slightly forward so that his hair fell across his face. I saw the fingers of his left hand moving over the strings. I sat up straighter to listen to him, but he broke off suddenly and a moment later I heard the lid of the violin case bang shut.

The next morning I saw the medicine bottle in the bathroom. I carefully removed the cork. It smelled bitter. I also noticed that it was no longer full. It was an ordinary bottle, like so many bottles in a medicine cabinet, except that this one didn't have a label. In the afternoon it still stood in the same spot, but it was now empty and the cork lay beside it. Just as I was heading down the stairs, my brother was coming up. At the top step he turned, went back down and came right back up again. He looked pale, and his face was beaded with sweat.

'Does it work fast?' I asked.

'Yes,' he mumbled, mounting the stairs again.

'Do you really have to climb up and down the stairs so much?'

'I really have to do all sorts of things,' he said, pausing at the top before dashing down to the bottom. 'Down is still easy,' he said, 'but up is already pretty hard.'

'How long are you going to keep at it?' I asked.

'We have to leave in a few minutes,' he said.

A long time went by before they came back.

'Maybe they're keeping them there,' said my mother.

'A lot of people have to be examined,' I said.

'As long as that bottle did its job,' said Lotte.

They came home a few hours later. Dave looked even sicker than before, but he as well as my father were in excellent spirits since they had both failed the physical.

'What did the doctor say?' Lotte wanted to know.

'Not much, but he found me unfit for a work camp,' said Dave. He lay down on the sofa. His hair was a mess and he had dark circles under his eyes.

A few years before I had once seen him lying around like that. He was a college student in Rotterdam at the time and, when my father paid him an unannounced visit, it turned out that my brother had been partying for more than a week and was in a constant state of drunkenness. My father took him home. 'All that drinking,' he'd said, 'is bound to ruin your health.'

My brother let his arm dangle limply down from the sofa; he had unbuttoned his shirt.

'All that from just a couple of drops,' he said.

The photos

The photos

After a few days Dave recovered from the adverse effects of the brown liquid. Lotte had run from the kitchen to the bedroom with delicious snacks and my mother had offered all sorts of advice.

'Give him plenty of milk. That always helps in cases like this,' she said, as if she had a world of experience.

'Let him rest,' said my father. But before long Dave was downstairs again, though he looked unwell for quite a while. Still, he went with us to the photographer to have his portrait made like everyone else.

Mrs Zwagers had started it. 'We've all had our photos taken,' she told my mother one afternoon when she came for tea. 'One of my husband and me, as well as one of the children. The thing is, it makes such a nice keepsake. You never know what will happen, but at least you'll have each other's photograph.'

My mother agreed. 'We should do it too,' she said. 'I think it's a good idea.'

'Let's all go to Smelting's,' said my father after my mother and he had discussed it. 'Make sure you look your best,' he said to us.

'I'm not photogenic,' I said. I didn't really feel like going with them.

'That's beside the point,' said my mother.

'Anyway,' I said, 'we have plenty of photos. A whole album.'

'Most of those are holiday snapshots,' said my mother. 'Taken years ago.'

'But they're nice,' I said. 'What's the use of such posed photographs!'

'Smelting makes very good portraits,' said my mother.

I ended up going with them even though I wasn't planning to have my picture taken. Lotte wore a new summer dress. She had carefully combed her blue-black hair into an upswept hairstyle. She and Dave posed together on Mr Smelting's sofa. 'Keep your eyes on my hand,' the photographer instructed them. He raised his hand and my brother and his wife looked at it.

'Now smile,' said Mr Smelting. They smiled simultaneously.

'Thank you,' he said. 'Who's next.'

My parents also stared at his hand. 'Feel free to smile as much as you can,' he said. 'People should look as cheerful as possible in a photo.'

'I'll come another time,' I said.

*

A busy time began for Mr Smelting. Word spread from one person to another. Friends kept dropping by to show us their portraits. They all looked the same. Everyone had looked at the hand and smiled.

One afternoon my mother set off to visit Mrs Zwagers so she could show her our photos. But she was back within half an hour, looking upset.

'They're gone!' she said. 'The entire Zwagers family has gone into hiding. I heard it from the neighbours. They left everything behind. I walked by the house. It looked as if they were still living there.'

It was the first time we'd heard that anyone had gone into hiding.

'Where could they have gone?' I asked.

'Somewhere in the countryside, of course,' said my mother. 'On a farm. She didn't breathe a word of it to me.'

'Of course she wouldn't,' said my father. 'You don't shout that sort of thing from the rooftops.'

'Imagine,' said my mother, 'leaving all your things behind.'

'When you go on holiday, you also leave your things behind,' I said.

'In that case at least you know when you'll come back,' said my mother. 'And they've got four children,' she continued, 'just think of all you'd need to take.'

'Going into hiding,' I said to my father. 'It strikes me as a kind of retreat from life.'

'Maybe they're right,' said my father. 'Who's to say?'

'I wish I could have shown them the photos,' said my mother. 'There's no telling how long they'll be gone.'

It happened

It happened

Slaves rule over us;
there is none who frees us from their hand.

Lamentations 5:8

I had always thought that nothing would ever happen to us, which is why I initially had trouble believing it was true. The morning the telegram arrived from Amsterdam, my first thought had been: someone has made a mistake. But that was not the case.

To get more information, my father and I went to the home of an acquaintance to make a phone call. This acquaintance was married to a midwife, who was not Jewish and was therefore allowed to keep her telephone for her work. She was in a dark backroom packing a small suitcase while my father was trying to get through to Amsterdam. I couldn't make out much of the phone conversation. My father gave short answers after long pauses, as if the person at the other end of the line were telling an elaborate story.

Meanwhile the midwife walked up and down the room, looked for something in a cupboard, went into another room, and came back. She was tall and blonde. She wore flat-heeled shoes that creaked at every step.

'They started taking people out of their homes on Merwedeplein,' said my father when the conversation had ended. He stood for a moment, still holding the receiver.

'I'll see you out,' said the midwife. She closed her suitcase, put on her coat, and led us into the hall. 'These are horrible times,' she said. 'And I'm up to my neck in work. It's all I can do to stay on top of things.'

'At nine o'clock in the evening they drove up to the front door in police vans,' said my father. He remained standing in the doorway, as if hesitating between the street and the room with the telephone.

'Is it your other daughter?' asked the midwife. My father nodded. The midwife pulled the door shut.

'How much do I owe you?' asked my father.

'Sixty cents,' she said. 'Most of them are daughters. People always think they're going to have a son, but it's usually a daughter.' She said goodbye and quickly got on her bike.

My father and I walked slowly in the other direction. He stared vacantly into space.

I saw it before me. I saw the big police vans and I saw my sister sitting inside.

'There isn't a thing we can do,' said my father. 'There's no one to offer a helping hand.'

I didn't know what to say. I felt exactly as I had years ago, when I saw my sister almost drown. We'd been staying with my grandparents in Twente and from there we had gone to the Dinkel River for the day. I was seven and Bettie, eight. My parents let us wade while they sat in the shade of a tree. We were picking flowers at the water's edge, when Bettie said, 'Look at the pretty ones on the other side.' She took a step toward them and I watched as she disappeared beneath the water. I stood there, rooted to the spot, staring at her arm, which could only be seen because she had clutched a clump of grass. My father jumped into the water fully clothed and was able to grab her hand just in the nick of time.

For the longest time I kept seeing her arm, sticking up out of the water. By then it had turned into a very different arm. I'd look at it when we were playing together or sitting at the table, but it no longer resembled her old arm.

We had reached our house. My father went inside. I remained in the front garden and sat down on the bench. The flowerbeds were filled with daffodils and tulips. I had picked some the day before and could see the cut stems. Inside, my father was relating how the police van had driven up to the front door.

There would be no point in sticking her arm out of that window now. If she did, it would be because it was crowded inside the van, for there was no one outside to offer her a helping hand.

Camping mugs

People told us, 'You should have been gone ages ago.' But we dismissed that. We stayed. I was now allowed to walk to my heart's content. Behind our house I had discovered a dirt road leading into woods where it was very quiet. Once in a while a farmer would pass by with milk cans. He'd look at the star on my coat and greet me warily, but he would have done that to anyone. Sometimes a scrawny dog walked beside me and a woman's shrill voice came from afar.

One day I came home from a walk and found three letters in the mailbox. Three yellow envelopes with our names in full as well as the dates of our birth. These were our call-ups, official notices to report for labour camps in the East.

'We have to report,' said Dave.

'I don't feel like it,' said Lotte. Everything in their house was still so new.

41

'We'll see something of the world. It might be exciting,' said Dave.

'It'll be a fantastic trip,' I said. 'I've never been farther than Belgium.'

We bought knapsacks and lined our clothes with fur and flannel. We crammed in as many boxes with vitamins as we could, since we had been told to bring them. The call-up notices also instructed us to take camping mugs. Dave was hoping to buy them downtown. I caught up with him just as he was about to turn the corner.

'I'll go with you,' I said. 'They won't be easy to find.'

'You think so?' asked Dave. 'We'll see.'

In the first shop we passed, we saw only ceramic mugs. 'Those are sure to get broken on the way,' said Dave. In the next shop they had camping mugs, but he found them too small. 'They'll hardly hold anything,' he said.

Finally, we came to a shop where they had the kind of mugs that Dave had in mind. They were large collapsible red mugs.

'What do you think we'll be using them for?' Dave asked me.

'All kinds of liquids, sir,' said the sales assistant. 'Milk and coffee, served hot, or wine and lemonade. These mugs are of excellent quality, the colour won't rub off, and they don't have a funny taste. Moreover, they're also guaranteed unbreakable.'

'We'll take three,' said Dave. 'Do they only come in red?'

'Yes,' said the assistant, 'only in red, but that's very cheerful for camping.'

'You're right,' said Dave. We left the shop, with Dave carrying the mugs that the assistant had wrapped into a neat package.

'Too bad that cafés and restaurants are off-limits to us,' he said, 'otherwise we could have had coffee somewhere in the city and tried out our new mugs.'

'They should be washed first,' I said.

On the way home we bumped into Mr Zaagmeier. 'We've bought mugs,' Dave told him. 'Three red camping mugs, one for each of us.'

'Did you get a call-up notice too?' asked Mr Zaagmeier. 'Oh dear, my son did as well. I'm on my way to see if anything can be done.'

'Why bother?' asked Dave. 'It won't do any good.'

'Come with me,' said Mr Zaagmeier. 'Do come with me. I know someone. Maybe he can arrange something for you too.'

'We've already packed,' I said.

Mr Zaagmeier took us to the man he knew.

'I'll help you,' the man said, 'provided you do exactly what I tell you to.'

'Too bad,' Dave said once again. 'We've already packed, sewn vitamins into every bit of clothing and we've just bought camping mugs.'

'If you go, you'll never come back,' said the man. 'Be sensible.'

'We'll get arrested if we don't report,' I said.

'Just do as I tell you,' said the man. 'Come to my place at nine o'clock this evening.'

Neither of us spoke on the way home, until Dave finally said, 'I don't understand why people are trying to scare us. What else will possibly happen to us?'

'Yes,' I said, 'what else?'

'And to think we could have seen something of the world,' he said.

Lotte was waiting for us in the front garden.

'You've been gone a long time,' she said. 'The doctor came by. He doesn't want you to leave now that you've barely recovered. He said you need to be careful. He's left you a medical certificate.'

'That settles it,' I said. 'None of us are going.'

'True,' said Dave, 'even though we've already bought camping mugs. Look.' He unwrapped them and set them on top of the gate of the front garden.

'What shall we do with them?' he asked.

Sealed

As it turned out, we didn't have to go to the man Mr Zaagmeier knew because Dave also received a medical certificate. Now there were two beds in the living room, and my brother and I walked around in our pyjamas all day so that we could leap into bed the moment the doorbell rang. Lotte was allowed to stay in order to take care of us but my parents were ordered to relocate to Amsterdam because they were over fifty.

It was a new regulation. They were permitted to take only one suitcase full of clothes and, before they left, both this suitcase and the room in which they'd been living had to be sealed.

'Have you forgotten anything?' asked my father.

'No, not a thing,' said my mother. She walked up and down the room, as if searching for something else to take. My father kept looking out the window.

'They were supposed to come before three,' he said. He checked his watch. 'It's already five minutes past three.'

'Do you think the suitcase will have to be opened again?' asked my mother.

'Of course not,' said my father. 'They won't have time to do all that. They'll just stick a seal on it, that's all. There they are.'

Two men in black leather jackets opened the gate and rang the bell. Dave and I were already in bed. Lotte answered the door and the two men came in without a word.

'Will that suitcase need to be opened?' I heard my mother say.

'That's what we've come for,' said one of the men.

I'd seen how carefully my mother had packed everything. Now they would turn it all upside down, as if they had lost something that was on the bottom. It reminded me of a trip to Belgium that we had taken shortly before the war. On the way home my mother had become very agitated. Every five minutes she asked my father if he thought the suitcase would have to be opened. At first I didn't understand what she was so worked up about. Only later, when the customs officer searched her suitcase, did I realise what the problem was. She had bought two large bottles of cologne and now had to pay import duties on them. So she might just as well have bought them in Holland.

When the men had gone, we examined the seals. 'It's child's play to loosen the seals and to slip more things into the suitcase,' I said. 'You could always glue them back on.' I picked at a corner. The seal did indeed come loose easily.

'Never mind,' said my father, 'we don't need anything else. Besides, we won't be away that long.'

His boundless optimism was contagious. I often asked him what he thought of the situation, only because I knew he would say something reassuring. When I got scared by people's stories about Poland, he always said, 'Things won't be that bad.' I never knew whether my father actually believed it or only said it to give us courage.

'Look,' he said, 'all the men are in the army, so of course they need young people to work in the war industry. Old people have to go and live in Amsterdam, where they'll set up a ghetto. It will become a large Jewish community.'

'Let's hope it won't last much longer,' said my mother. I knew she was thinking of Bettie. *'I'm fine,'* Bettie had written on a postcard that we received from her a few days after the round-up. *'Please don't worry.'*

If it didn't last too long, she'd be able to survive in Poland. 'She's strong and healthy,' everyone said. 'She'll get through it somehow.'

After my parents had left, Lotte and I stood in the hall for a while staring at the seal on the door frame. It gave the room a mysterious air, as if there were something hidden that we weren't allowed to see.

'Let's go in,' said Lotte. She ran her nail down the crack, splitting the seal in half. We felt as if we were entering an unfamiliar room. Carefully, as if someone might hear us, we walked around the table, ran our hands over a chair, a cupboard.

'Those men have made a list of everything in here,' whispered Lotte. 'We can no longer remove anything.'

I moved a small vase. 'It also feels like it's no longer ours,' I whispered back. 'Why do you think that is?'

'Because they've put their filthy hands on everything,' said Lotte.

We left the room as it was, torn seal and all.

In safekeeping

'How you managed to put up with staying in bed for so many months is a mystery to me,' Dave said. We'd been walking around in pyjamas for weeks now and sometimes stayed in bed all day because we'd heard so many rumours about sudden house checks.

'Oh well,' I said, 'you do what you have to.'

'True,' he said. 'And of course you get used to it. Like you get used to wearing a yellow star and not having a radio.'

'Except that in the hospital I felt it was for my own good,' I said.

Suddenly I heard a voice shouting from outside. 'Hey, can I borrow your racket?' The garden doors were open. The neighbour's daughter stuck her head up above the fence, smiled and peered inside.

'Sure,' I shouted back.

She climbed over the fence and jumped into our garden.

'Terrific,' she said, brushing some sand off her full, flowered skirt.

'I don't need it,' I said. 'You can have it.'

'Of course you're not playing tennis these days, are you?' she said.

'No,' said Dave, 'not now. Tennis courts are off-limits for the likes of us.'

'Anyway,' she said to me, 'the doctor wouldn't have let you play.'

'You're right,' I said. 'Come on in and we'll go to my room.'

We went upstairs. While I was looking in the cupboard for my racket, the girl was checking out my books. 'Would you look at that!' she said.

I turned around. I thought she meant a book, but she held out a ceramic kitten. 'Go ahead and take it,' I said. 'After all, we won't be able to stay here much longer.'

'I'd love to,' she said. 'It would be a pity to leave all these pretty things here.'

'That's true,' I said. 'Feel free to take something else.'

She walked around the room and picked up a small vase, a little wooden bowl, an old copper box and a few other tiny things.

'Oh,' she exclaimed, 'look at that handbag!' She set the things she was holding down on the table and snatched up the handbag that was hanging on a chair. She inspected it carefully, opening it, and taking out everything that was inside.

'Here,' she said, 'I'll empty it entirely. It's gorgeous.'

'It's my sister's,' I said. 'She made it herself.'

'Was she that good at leatherwork?' she asked.

'She made lots of things out of leather, all very beautiful.'

'I'll keep it for you,' she said.

'OK,' I said.

'It's all right if I use it every once in a while, isn't it?'

'Sure,' I said. 'Go ahead.'

She stood there, cradling the racket, the handbag and the other items in her arms and casting her eyes around the room as if she'd forgotten something.

'That tile. . .' she said.

I took it off the wall and placed it on top of the other things.

'Here, let me get the door for you,' I said.

'I should have brought a bag,' she said, smiling.

'But of course you didn't know you'd have to carry so many things. After all, you only came to get the racket, didn't you?'

'That's right,' she said. 'Nice of you to let me use yours. It's a good racket, isn't it? I just thought I'd ask. It's a pity to let it lie in the cupboard. Besides, it'll be a while before you people are allowed to play tennis again.'

I accompanied her down the stairs and held the front door open for her. 'Can you manage?' I asked.

'Oh yes,' she said, then paused hesitantly on the mat. 'Would you check if anyone's coming?' she asked. 'You have to be so careful nowadays . . . If anyone saw me leaving your house . . . You never know . . . It would create a whole lot of unnecessary trouble.'

I threw my coat on over my pyjamas and looked down the street, first to the left, then to the right.

'The coast is clear,' I said.

'Well then, bye-bye,' she said. She bounded out the gate and ran into the front garden of the house next door with the handbag dangling from her arm and the tail of the ceramic kitten sticking out of it.

Homecoming

'Guess what I'm going to do?' I said to my brother one afternoon. 'I'm going to Amsterdam.'

'Whatever gave you that idea?' said his wife. 'It seems very foolish.'

'I'm fed up,' I said. 'I'd like to wear regular clothes again.'

'I know what you mean,' said Dave. 'It might be best for you to be in Amsterdam. We should go there too.'

'But how will you do it?' asked Lotte.

'I'll just take the star off my coat and board the train. Very simple.'

'As long as there isn't a strict checkpoint,' said Dave.

'I'll be careful,' I said. 'I'm going, no matter what.'

I wanted to visit my parents. They had written that they'd been lucky enough to find rooms in a large house with a garden on Sarphatistraat. 'We've already met several people we know,' wrote my father. 'We all live in the same neighbourhood.' Although I could tell from their letters that their lives were not unpleasant, I realised they would prefer one of their children to be with them. Especially now that they were so worried about Bettie. Nothing more had been heard from her after the one postcard.

I planned to leave as soon as it got dark. I was as excited as a child who is allowed to travel for the first time. Not because I'd soon see my parents, but because I could pretend, if only for a short while, that everything was normal. On the way to the station, however, I thought I saw a policeman checking people's papers on every street corner. And in the dimly lit station I imagined that everyone was looking at me with suspicion.

In the train I sat huddled in a corner next to a woman rocking her child to sleep on her lap. The man across from me smoked a pipe and stared out the window, though there was nothing to see. As we rode through the dark landscape, I forgot my fear and began to enjoy myself. I couldn't resist humming to the monotonous rhythm of the wheels. I remembered how Bettie and I used to spend our holidays in Amsterdam when we were small. Then in the train we'd try to outdo each other in coming up with a rhyme that matched the rhythm of the wheels. 'To-ám-ster-dam-and-rótter-dam-with-búttered-bread-and-bér-ry-jam,' we'd sometimes drone on for miles on end.

Amsterdam was dark and wet. There were still a fair number of people on the streets. They moved like shadows on the broad pavements of Damrak. No one looked at me. No one followed me. I had trouble finding the house on Sarphatistraat because it was so dark underneath the trees. I kept having to climb steep flights of steps to read the numbers on doors until I finally found the right house. It was set back a bit from the street. I already had my hand on the bell when I realised that I couldn't ring it just like that. It would scare everyone in the house. So I tried whistling, but no one seemed to hear me. I had no choice but to ring the bell. I did it cautiously, three times in a row. The moment I heard someone in the hall, I shouted my name through the letter box.

'Is that you?' said my father, surprised. He opened the door a crack to let me in.

'I've come to take a look,' I said cheerfully.

'Good heavens,' said my mother. 'I can't believe you dared to come.'

'Nothing to it,' I said.

The other residents came in – after ascertaining that nothing serious was going on – to gawk at me.

'Did you sit in the train, just like that?' one of them asked.

'Didn't anyone ask for your identity card?' asked another.

'How did you ever dare to buy a ticket at the window?'

They looked at the blank spot on my coat where the star had been, as if it were a rare sight.

'I can still see a few yellow threads,' someone said.

'You'd better sew it back on,' said my mother.

'Was it crowded in the train?' asked my father.

They grilled me as if I'd made a long journey, as if I'd come from a foreign country.

'You must be hungry,' said my mother. She left the room and came back with a couple of sandwiches.

Though I wasn't the least bit hungry, I dug into one so I wouldn't disappoint my mother.

They all remained standing around the table, watching me with a look of such genuine satisfaction that I forced myself to polish off the sandwiches until not a single crumb was left.

In the basement

The house on Sarphatistraat was a gloomy place. The rooms were high-ceilinged, covered with dark wallpaper and furnished with decent but heavy furniture.

A week after my parents moved in, the family that owned the house suddenly disappeared. My parents sat waiting for them in vain at the breakfast table one morning. At first they thought that the owners had overslept, but when they failed to appear, they concluded that the family had decided it would be wiser to leave the troubled city. Together with the family that had likewise only recently come to live on the upper floor, my parents agreed that they would use the entire lower floor. By the time I arrived, my mother had adapted well to the new situation and arranged the rooms to suit her own taste, so that I was reminded of our house in Breda. And yet, with its narrow hallways, dark stairs, and brown doors, it was still a house typical of Amsterdam. A steep spiral staircase led to a basement filléd with furniture, lampshades, bolts of silk, and boxes crammed with beads and trimmings.

After discovering that treasure trove, I spent hours in the basement, poking around the musty fabric, the gold-embroidered ribbons and the cold metal frameworks of the lampshades. As a child I had often rummaged through a chest filled with carnival costumes in the attic, trying them all on and spending entire afternoons walking around in them. In the same way I draped myself with strings of beads and strolled through the damp basement.

One morning my father came down the stairs with his coat on and my coat draped over his arm.

'Hurry, put it on,' he said. My mother came down behind him. I immediately flung aside the beads while my father switched off the light. We sat down in the semi-darkness by the barred window on the street side of the house, where only the feet of passers-by were visible. At first, no one went past. But after a few minutes we saw big black boots that made a loud, clicking noise. They emerged from the house on our right and crossed over to the kerb, where a car was waiting. We also saw ordinary shoes walking beside the boots: brown men's shoes, a pair of pumps with worn-down heels, and gym shoes. Two pairs of boots walked slowly toward the car, as if they were carrying something heavy.

'Lots of people live in the house next door,' whispered my father. 'It's a rest home and quite a few of the residents are ill.'

A pair of beige children's boots stopped in front of our window. The toes faced slightly in, and the laces of one boot were darker than those of the other.

'That's Liesje,' my mother said softly. 'She's growing so fast. Those boots are already much too small for her.'

The child lifted her foot and, as if she were hopping, that one small boot jumped back and forth in front of our window.

Until it was joined by a pair of black boots. We heard the door of the house on our right slam shut. The boots stayed put. They were well-polished, had unworn heels, and had planted themselves firmly in front of our window. We gazed at the scene as if it were a shop window with a special display. My mother craned her head a bit so she could see around the bar that was blocking her view, while my father looked straight ahead.

The boots started to move and we watched as first the left one took a step forward, then the right one, then the left, the right, moving away from the window, toward the left.

The doorbell rang in the house on our left. We stayed where we were until we no longer saw any boots. Then we went upstairs and hung our coats on the coat rack.

Sabbath

By looking over the edge of my mother's prayer book –
where she was tracing the letters with her fingers so I
could follow along – and peering down through the lat-
ticed screen, I could see my father in his prayer shawl, his
tallit. I couldn't help thinking of the *shul* in Breda, which
was much smaller and not nearly as beautiful. But there
my father had a roomy pew all to himself, which looked
just like a coach without wheels. To get out of it, he had
to open a little round door and go down a few steps. The
door creaked and, when I heard it, I'd look down and
watch my father proceed to the middle of the sanctuary.
I followed his shiny top hat and his ample *tallit*, which
would flutter a little behind him as he walked. He climbed
the steps of the *almemor* – the raised platform where the
Torah was read and where he was called upon to distribute
mitzvoth, blessings. Then I would suddenly hear our names
called between the half-chanted Hebrew texts. Our

names sounded very beautiful in Hebrew and they were longer because my father's name was always added to them. Then my mother would also look down through the screen and smile at my father. The women in the gallery would nod at my mother as a sign they'd heard the names and would wait to see if their husbands would give them a *mitzvah* so that my mother could nod at *them* in return. It was a custom in the Breda Jewish community.

But now, in this *shul*, I saw my father sitting in a pew somewhere toward the back, among the other men. He was wearing his everyday hat and he stayed in his seat until the end of the service. It was a long service. Special prayers were said for the Jews in the camps. Some of the women cried. The woman in front of me sat huddled over her prayer book and blew her nose repeatedly. She was wearing a reddish-brown wig that had slid back under her hat. My mother had set her prayer book next to her on the bench and was gazing fixedly into space. I put my hand on her arm.

'It's very cold in Poland now,' she whispered.

'But she was able to take warm clothes with her, wasn't she?' I said softly. 'She had her knapsack all packed and was ready to go.'

My mother nodded. Just then the cantor started another prayer, so we all stood up. Down below a Torah scroll had been taken out of the Holy Ark. The scroll was clad in purple velvet and had a silver crown from which hung little bells that tinkled when the Torah was being carried around the synagogue. The men kissed a corner of the velvet cover as the Torah went by. After a while the congregation broke out in the closing song of the service. It's a cheerful melody that surprises me every time because it begins so exuberantly. While they sang, the men folded up their prayer shawls and the women donned their coats. I watched as my father carefully put away his prayer shawl in the small *tallit* bag.

In front of the building people waited for one another, shaking hands and wishing each other a 'good Shabbos'. My father was already there when my mother and I came out. As a child, I hated having to walk home afterwards with the others, since I was always afraid I'd run into kids from my school.

Most people dispersed quickly across the square. Some went in the direction of Weesperstraat, others toward Waterlooplein. One of my father's acquaintances asked if we'd walk part of the way down Nieuwe Amstelstraat with him.

'I've sent my wife and children to the countryside,' he said. 'At least for now they're better off there than here.'

'Why didn't you go with them?' asked my mother.

'Oh no,' he said, 'it wouldn't suit me at all. I'm managing just fine.'

'So are you living on your own now?' asked my mother.

'No,' he said, 'with my sister. She hasn't decided yet what to do either.'

'What choices are there?' said my father.

'Well,' said his acquaintance, 'you could shut the door behind you and simply disappear. But what would you live on?'

'Exactly,' said my father. 'You have to live. You have to support yourself somehow.'

We were standing on the corner by the Amstel River, with an icy wind blowing in our faces. My father's acquaintance shook our hands. 'My sister's place is that way,' he said and crossed the bridge to Amstelstraat. A small, hunched-over figure in a black coat with an upturned collar, clutching his hat. We walked along the Amstel, crossing the bridge at Nieuwe Herengracht and passing under the yellow sign with '*Judenviertel/* Jewish Quarter' written across it in black letters. A couple of children wearing woollen mufflers were leaning over the railing and throwing pieces of bread to the seagulls, who caught them deftly as they skimmed over the water. A police van drove down the other side of the street and a woman thrust open a window and shouted something to the children, who dropped the rest of the bread and ran inside.

'Let's take the shortest way home,' said my mother. So we went along the canal.

'We'll be home in no time,' said my father.

'I hear that more and more people are going into hiding,' I said.

'Yes,' said my father, 'we're going to try and find something for you, too.'

'No,' I said, 'I won't go by myself.'

'It would be easier if we still lived in Breda,' said my mother. 'We'd have a place in no time. We don't know anyone here.'

'There we might have been able to stay with neighbours,' I said.

'Or in any number of places, for that matter,' said my mother. 'We had friends everywhere.'

'It costs so much money here,' said my father. 'How am I supposed to come up with that kind of money?'

'If only we knew more people,' said my mother.

'Let's wait and see,' said my father. 'Maybe it won't be necessary. And if it isn't, then you're stuck being with strangers and causing them trouble.'

We had reached our house. My father stuck the key in the lock. Instinctively I looked up and down the street before going in. The heater was on in the living room, and the table was set. My mother had seen to that before we left. My father went off to wash his hands. Then he stood with us at the table, removed the embroidered cloth from the Sabbath challah, tore off the end and divided it into three pieces that he dipped in salt while reciting a prayer. I mumbled a *bracha* and ate the salty crust.

'This is good,' said my father as he took his seat.

The girl

One Friday afternoon my mother sent me out to do some shopping. 'Just go to Weesperstraat,' she said. 'You'll find everything you need there.'

Aunt Kaatje was coming to dinner. My father had to collect her from the old folks' home since she could no longer go out by herself. She was over eighty and was the twin sister of my grandmother, who had died several years before the war. She was delighted whenever my father picked her up to eat with us, for then she could talk about the past, about the time when her husband was still alive. At around the turn of the century she had made numerous trips to foreign countries and could still remember every detail. Since she didn't have any children, she had gone to live in the home after her husband died. Her biggest regret was not being able to travel any more.

'There's still a chance I'll take another trip once the war is over,' she said once when she was visiting.

'Aunt Kaatje loves shortbread,' said my mother. 'Don't forget to pick some up.'

I promised not to forget anything. While I was putting on my coat, my mother came into the hall.

'Come back soon,' she said. 'It gets dark so early.'

My mother used to tell me the same thing years ago when she let me play outside before dinner – except that now she said it for a different reason.

I had just pulled the door shut behind me when a fat man came up to me. It was as if he'd been waiting for me and knew I'd be leaving the house at that particular moment. He positioned himself right in front of me so I couldn't get away.

'What's your name?' he asked.

I gave him my name. He had a double chin, red-veined cheeks and dark bags under his watery eyes.

'Humph,' he said. 'Do you expect me to believe that?'

'But it *is* my name,' I said.

'Pretty quick with the answers, aren't you?' he said. 'Like all you people. Where are you going?'

'Shopping,' I said, and started to walk off.

'Hold your horses,' he said. 'Stay right where you are.'

I glanced at the people going by, but no one paid attention to us. It was as if we were just standing there, talking.

'What's your name?' he asked again.

I gave it to him once more. He curled his upper lip. He had brown teeth and the ones in front were crooked.

'How old are you?' he asked.

I told him how old I was.

'That's correct,' he said. He held out his hand. 'Your identity card.'

I was surprised that it had taken him this long to ask me for it. I took the card out of my bag. He snatched it from my fingers and inspected it carefully.

'Hmm,' he said, 'I'm looking for a different girl.'

He mentioned a name I hadn't heard before. 'Do you know her? She's supposedly living in this neighbourhood.'

'No,' I said, 'I don't know her.'

'Are you sure?' he insisted. He moved even closer. There were ash smudges on his lapels and his tie was crooked.

'I don't know her,' I repeated and took a step backward.

'Humph,' he growled and gave me back my identity card. 'Now off you go!'

I started walking and didn't dare look back until I reached Weesperplein. He was still standing in the same spot. I wondered who the girl was. Perhaps I'd seen her sometime, perhaps we'd passed each other on Sarphatistraat.

It was busy on Weesperstraat. Inside the tiny shops women with shopping bags were stocking up before the Sabbath. Salesgirls and bosses in white overalls – with pencils jutting out of the breast pockets onto which a yellow star had been sewn – were bustling around behind the counters. People laughed at the jesting remark of a fat lady with a bulging bag of groceries. Two small boys in navy-blue jackets peered into the window of a sweet shop. Their yellow stars had been sewn on so low that it looked like their pockets had little windmills that might start turning at any moment. I quickly finished my shopping and hurried back home. This time I walked along Achtergracht, which was a quieter street. An old woman holding a white handkerchief in front of her mouth was just going into the hospital on the corner, helped by two men.

Aunt Kaatje would have arrived at our house by now. It would make her happy to hear that I'd bought the shortbread on Weesperstraat. 'The best shortbread in the world comes from Weesperstraat,' she always said. And we believed her because she was sure to know.

When I turned the corner of Roetersstraat, I saw that the fat man had gone. I was planning to ask my mother if she knew who the girl was, but she had a worried look on her face when she met me in the hall.

'Aunt Kaatje is gone,' she said. 'The entire old folks' home has been cleared out.'

'All those old people have been hauled away?' I asked.

My mother nodded. I handed her my bag with the groceries. Well, I thought as I went into the living room, Aunt Kaatje had looked forward to another trip. My father told us what he'd heard from the people living near the home.

Only hours later did I think again of the girl who was my age, the girl I didn't know.

Lepelstraat

As I turned onto Lepelstraat, I saw a police van approaching at the far end of the street. Men in helmets and green uniforms were sitting stiffly on two rows of benches. The van stopped and the men leaped out. I turned around to retrace my steps, but an identical van had already driven into the street behind me. The men inside it were likewise sitting perfectly still and erect, like tin soldiers in a toy car. They simultaneously leaped out of both sides of the van, strode over to the houses and pushed open the doors, most of which had been left ajar so they wouldn't have to be broken down. One of the soldiers came up to me and ordered me to get into the van, which at this point was still empty.

'I don't live here,' I said.

'Get in anyway,' said the man in the green uniform.

I didn't move. 'No,' I repeated clearly. 'I don't live on Lepelstraat. Ask your commanding officer whether you're also supposed to round up people who live on another street.'

He turned and walked over to the officer, who was standing a few feet away from the van, keeping an eye on his men. The soldier spoke to him briefly, pointing at me a couple of times as he did so. I didn't move from where I was and saw a little boy suddenly emerge from a door near me. He was carrying a knapsack in one hand and a slice of bread with molasses in the other. There was a brown smear on his chin. From an open door I heard heavy steps on a staircase. The soldier came back and asked for my identity card, which he took over to the officer, who looked at it, muttered something and gave it back to the soldier. Holding the card in the same hand that was also clutching the gun, the soldier approached me again. He walked slower this time and stepped on a piece of paper that was being blown across the pavement. His helmet came down to his eyebrows, making his forehead look like it was made out of green steel. Meanwhile the little boy in the doorway had eaten his bread and tied his knapsack onto his back.

The soldier handed me my identity card and told me I could go. I walked past the van, where several women were now sitting on the benches. An old woman carrying a brown blanket was climbing in awkwardly, but the man behind her gave her a push. Somewhere a door was being pounded and a window was slammed shut.

When I reached Roetersstraat, I broke into a run and kept running until I was home.

'That was fast!' said my mother. 'Didn't you go to the butcher's shop?'

'No,' I said, 'I couldn't.'

'Was it closed?' asked my mother.

'No,' I said, 'Lepelstraat was blocked off.'

The next morning I walked through Lepelstraat again. Papers were scattered everywhere and doors were standing wide open. A grey cat was sitting on the steps of a dark stairwell. When I stopped, it ran to the top of the stairs and glared at me with its back arched. A child's glove lay on one of the steps. A few houses away a door with a splintered panel hung out of its hinges, and the mailbox was suspended crookedly from a nail with the mail sticking out of it. I couldn't tell whether it was printed matter or letters. Curtains fluttered out of a number of windows. Somewhere a flowerpot lay upturned, on the edge of a windowsill. Behind another window I saw a table that had already been set: a piece of bread on a plate and a slab of butter with a knife stuck in it. The butcher's shop where I was supposed to get meat the day before was empty. A plank had been hammered across the door, so that no one could enter. Someone must have done that early in the day. The butcher's shop looked nice and clean from the outside, as if the butcher had first given it a thorough cleaning. The shutter in front of the tiny pickle seller's shop was closed, though the vinegary smell of the pickle barrels was still in the air. From under the shutter a trail of pickle juice ran across the pavement into the gutter, most likely from barrels that had toppled. A sudden gust of wind sent papers whirling across the asphalt and slamming against the houses. Right next to me a door fell shut, though no one came out. A shutter banged back and forth. And it was not yet evening.

Just as I was about to turn the corner, I saw something on a doorpost – the red eye on the enamelled plate of the night security service.

The door was standing wide open.

The men

The evening the men came I fled through the garden gate. It had been a mild spring day. In the afternoon we had lounged in the garden in deckchairs, and in the evening I noticed that my face was a bit sunburned.

My mother had been sick all week, and that afternoon, feeling somewhat better, she lay in the sun.

'Tomorrow I'll start knitting you a summer sweater,' she promised me. My father lay silently smoking a cigar, the book on his lap closed.

In the garden shed I had found a tennis racket and a ball and began practising against the wall. The ball kept flying over it, which meant I had to open the garden gate and go look for it in the street. Sometimes the ball ended up behind the fence. Between our garden and our neighbours' there was a narrow ditch with a fence on either side. You could stand almost upright in it without being seen.

While I was searching for the ball, my father came over to take a look.

'That'd be a nice hiding place,' he said.

He climbed over the fence and we crouched behind a tree that belonged to neither us nor the neighbours. Our feet sank into the soft soil that smelled of rotting leaves. While we sat there, hidden by the semidarkness, my father gave a short whistle.

'Hello!' he then called out.

'Where are you?' asked my mother. Apparently, she had dozed off.

'Can you see us?' my father called out.

'No,' my mother answered, 'where are you?'

'Here,' said my father, 'behind the fence. Look closely.'

We peeked through a crack and saw my mother coming nearer.

'I still can't see you,' she said.

'Good,' said my father. He straightened up and jumped nimbly over the fence.

'Stay where you are,' he said to me, then motioned to my mother to try and climb over it too.

'Why should I?' she asked.

'Just try it,' he said.

My mother had to do it again several times before my father felt that she was doing it smoothly. Then he climbed over the fence himself and the three of us crouched in the ditch.

'No one would think to look for us here,' he said. 'Let's stay here for a while to see how long we can remain in this position.'

But I discovered my ball among the leaves. 'I'm going to practise my backhand,' I exclaimed and jumped into the garden.

My father and mother remained in the ditch.

'Can you see us?' yelled my father.

'No,' I yelled back, 'I can't see a thing.' They then reappeared. My mother dusted herself off.

'I'm absolutely filthy,' she said.

'Tomorrow I'll hollow it out a little more and rake away the leaves so we can sit more comfortably,' said my father.

That evening, after dinner, I stood by the window and looked outside. There wasn't a soul in the street. It was so quiet that you could hear the birds singing.

'Please move away from the window,' said my mother.

'There's nothing to see,' I said. Still, I turned around and sat down. My mother poured tea, moving quietly between my father and me and the tea table.

'Perhaps it would be better if we didn't drink tea,' said my father. 'Then, if they do come, we can go more quickly into the garden.'

'It's so dreary without tea,' observed my mother.

Darkness slowly fell. While my father was drawing the curtains, the first trucks rumbled past. He stood there, still holding the curtain, and looked at us.

'There they go,' he said.

'They're passing our house,' said my mother. We listened to the sounds outside. The engine roar receded and for a while all was still. Then we heard cars driving down the street again. This time it took longer for things to quieten down. But then there fell a silence that we hardly dared to break. I saw my mother looking at her half-full teacup and knew she wanted to drink it. And yet she didn't move a muscle.

After some time, my father said, 'Let's wait ten more minutes and then we'll turn on the overhead light.' But before those ten minutes were up, the bell rang. It was just before nine. We remained seated and looked at one another in surprise. As if we wondered: Who could that be? As if we didn't know! As if we thought: It could simply be a friend dropping by for a visit! After all, it was early in the evening, and the tea was ready.

They must have had a master key.

They were standing in the room before we were able to make the slightest move. They were big men and they were wearing light raincoats.

'Get our coats, please,' my father said to me.

My mother finished her tea.

With my coat on, I remained standing in the hall. I heard my father say something and one of the men say something back, though I couldn't make out the words. I listened with my ear pressed against the living room door. Again I heard my father's voice and again I couldn't hear what he said. Then I turned around, walked through the kitchen and went into the garden. It was dark. My foot bumped against something round. It must have been a ball.

I closed the garden gate softly behind me, ran down the street, and kept running until I came to Frederiksplein. There was no one to be seen, only a dog sniffing its way past the houses. I crossed the square. I felt as if I were alone in a deserted city.

Bitter herbs

The first few days I blamed myself for having abandoned my parents. I couldn't help feeling that it would have been better if I'd stayed with them. I had run out through the garden gate without thinking. It wasn't until I was standing in front of the house on Weteringschans, where my brother had gone into hiding a few days earlier, that I considered turning back. Just then, however, the clock in the church tower struck the curfew hour. I rang the bell.

'You did the right thing,' said Dave. 'You couldn't have done anything else.'

'But they'll wonder where I am,' I said. 'They'll be worried.'

'They'll understand,' said Dave. 'They're just happy you got away.'

'I could wait in front of the Hollandsche Schouwburg where they're being held,' I suggested. 'They might see me when they're being brought out.' But Dave wouldn't let me. He thought it was far too risky.

From our neighbours on Sarphatistraat we heard that ever since my escape someone had been keeping an eye on the house all day long. Because they now had my identity card, they also knew what I looked like; and because all my clothes were still hanging there, they assumed I'd come and get them.

So before venturing outside again, I underwent a metamorphosis. First Lotte bleached my hair. I sat in front of the mirror with a sheet wrapped around me, while she applied a mixture of hydrogen peroxide and ammonia with a toothbrush. It stung my scalp and caused my eyes to water, so that I was constantly blinking like a child struggling to hold back its tears. I tried to follow the process of my hair discolouring in the mirror, but all I could see was the white foam of the peroxide that smarted and hissed. After being washed and dried, my hair was red. But Lotte assured me that I would turn blonde after several more applications. I plucked my eyebrows until only thin lines were left. There was no longer anything dark about my appearance. Since I have blue eyes, the bleached hair matched my complexion better than it did Lotte's. She had dark brown, almost black eyes with long blue-black lashes, which made her blonde hair look unnatural.

At first we thought that nothing more could happen to us. We now had fake identity cards, which made us feel like 'ordinary' people. Yet we never felt totally safe on the street. Whenever we saw a policeman, we expected him to make a beeline toward us and it seemed as if every passer-by looked at us and knew what we were. In the end, Mrs K., the woman Dave had rented a room from under a false name, realised it as well.

'Are you and your sister-in-law so enamoured of bleached hair?' she asked when she saw me changed from one day to the next.

'We think it's terrific,' I said. 'Not to mention that we have a really good dye that doesn't harm your hair in the least.'

She might not have given it another thought if Dave hadn't bleached his hair as well. He had emptied the entire bottle over his head. It wasn't a very smart thing to do because it's impossible for a man to maintain a dye job and after a few weeks Dave's hair would start looking notice-ably peculiar.

'You too now?' observed Mrs K. with feigned amiability.

'My husband accidentally poured peroxide on his hair instead of shampoo,' explained Lotte.

Mrs K. laughed heartily. 'I wondered,' she said.

That evening she asked us over for tea. She was having company and it would be nice if we could join them. Later it turned out that her guest, a plump man with shrewd eyes, had been invited in order to size us up and confirm her suspicions.

After we'd gone back to our room, she stuck her head around the door. 'It would be better if you moved out early tomorrow morning,' she informed us. Out in the hall the man put on his coat and whistled as he went down the stairs.

'I know about a place in Utrecht,' Dave said. 'I'm sure we can stay there.'

'I hope so,' said Lotte, 'because where else would we go?'

'Plenty of doors are still open to us,' declared Dave.

I couldn't help thinking of those doors when I lay in bed that night and couldn't sleep. I thought about the door that I had always been allowed to open on the evening of the Seder so that the weary stranger could see that he was welcome and would join us at our table. Every year I hoped that someone would come in, but no one ever did.

I also thought about the questions that I, as the youngest child, had to ask. '*Ma nishtanah halaila hazeh.* Why is this night different from all other nights, and why do we eat unleavened bread and bitter herbs . . .?'

Then, in a lilting voice, my father would recount the story of the Exodus from Egypt, and we would eat the unleavened bread and the bitter herbs so that we would be reminded of their bitterness to the length of days.

Separated

The three of us had agreed to wait for each other in a second-class compartment of the train to Utrecht. We had gone to the station together, but had bought tickets at different windows and passed the checkpoint separately.

Earlier, as we were strolling down Damrak, Lotte had suggested going to a movie. It had been a long time since we'd seen one. We were able to relax a bit in the dark theatre, where no one asked for your papers and where outward differences were scarcely noticeable. In front of me sat a big man whose back blocked my view, but it didn't matter. Dave and Lotte weren't paying much attention to the movie either. Of course it was a German movie, but the three of us weren't really following the story.

When we came out of the cinema, it was time for us to take the train. As we neared the station, Dave said, 'It's better if we separate now. Let's wait for each other in the second-class compartment.'

'Isn't that awfully complicated?' I asked. 'Wouldn't it be easier to buy all three tickets at the same time?'

'No,' said Dave, 'it's better this way.'

'But,' I persisted, 'wouldn't you rather go into the station together? If anything happens, at least we'll be together.'

'Nothing's going to happen,' said my brother. He stepped away from us and entered the station. Lotte and I did as he had instructed us. I picked a window where the others weren't standing, went through the checkpoint and looked for the train to Utrecht.

There were still seven minutes to go. Since all the window seats on the platform side of the train were taken, I couldn't watch out for Dave and Lotte. I had expected them to get in soon after me. I hadn't seen a special checkpoint anywhere. And yet there was no sign of them.

'This *is* the train to Utrecht, isn't it?' I asked a woman across from me. Perhaps I hadn't looked carefully and had boarded the wrong train. But the woman confirmed that it was the train to Utrecht.

'Utrecht is a nice city,' she added. 'Don't you think so?' I nodded.

'Of course, it's no match for Amsterdam,' she continued, 'but I like being there anyway. It has an intimacy that I sometimes miss in Amsterdam.'

'Yes,' I said, 'that's true.' I saw a few passengers still getting in. My brother and his wife were not among them.

'Besides,' said the woman across from me, 'my whole family lives there and of course that makes a difference. Do you have family in Utrecht too?'

'No,' I said.

'Oh, then you must have friends there,' she said. 'I do too, very good friends, who used to live in Amsterdam.'

One minute before the train was due to leave my brother entered the compartment. He didn't sit down and didn't look at me. He set his bag down next to me and was gone before I could ask him anything. The train started to move immediately afterwards, as if he'd been the one to give the departure signal.

'Is that your bag?' asked the woman.

'Yes,' I said, 'I'd forgotten it.'

'Nice of that gentleman to bring it to you,' she said.

We had passed the houses of the eastern part of the city, and the train was now leaving Amsterdam at full speed.

'Well,' said the woman, 'it's only a hop, skip and a jump. We'll be there in no time.'

But I thought it took a long time. I had placed the bag on my lap and was staring outside. As we approached Utrecht, I got up and went into the corridor.

'Have a good time in Utrecht today,' the woman called after me. Her words stuck in my head when I crossed the square in front of the station. I still heard them as I turned the corner, walked down a broad shopping street and passed a cafeteria that reeked of grease. I paused in front of the window of a shoe shop, feeling so nauseated that I was afraid I was going to throw up. 'Breathe deeply, that will keep it down where it belongs,' the nurse in the hospital used to say to me when I was similarly affected during my treatment. I took several deep breaths and that helped.

A moment later I was standing in the doorway of the house where I was supposed to be. 'It's above a grocery,' Dave had told me that morning. The door opened the minute I rang the bell. I started up the stairs. It was a steep staircase with a maroon runner. A tiny light bulb was burning on the first landing. Some of the carpet rods on the flight of stairs had come loose and this flight was even longer and steeper than the first one. I saw a man and a woman standing at the top. They looked at me without saying a word.

'I'm . . .' I started.

'We know,' said the man. 'Your brother called us from the station and told us you'd be coming alone.'

'Did he tell you anything else?' I asked.

'Yes,' said the man. 'He said that his wife had been detained at the checkpoint. He was going to join her as soon as he hung up.'

I followed them into the living room, where they pointed to a deep chair.

'I'm very sorry,' said the man, 'I don't have enough room for you here, but I do have another address you could go to.'

The woman set a cup of tea in front of me. I was still holding my brother's bag, so I put it on my lap and took a sip of tea.

The crossroad

That same evening I went back to Amsterdam.

'You're welcome to spend the night here,' they told me in Utrecht. But I didn't want to. I wanted to go back to Amsterdam right away. They urged me to at least have a bite to eat or rest for a while. But I wasn't tired and I wasn't hungry. Instead I phoned an acquaintance in Amsterdam.

'Just come here,' said Wout. I had met him some weeks earlier at the house of a Jewish family. My parents were already gone. 'Call me if you're ever in trouble,' he'd said. I hadn't given him another thought.

A few hours later I boarded the train with my brother's bag. This time I didn't worry about checkpoints, I didn't keep an eye out for policemen or soldiers, I didn't look for a particular compartment. A lot of my fear had fallen away. If I were caught now, at least I would no longer feel I'd be left behind, all alone.

Wout was waiting for me at the Amstelstation. 'I've arranged things with Uncle Hannes,' he said. 'He'll pick you up tomorrow morning.'

I didn't ask who Uncle Hannes was. It sounded as if he was talking about one of my uncles, and I left it at that.

'Is that bag all you have?' asked Wout.

'I have a suitcase with some clothes,' I said, 'but it's still at the house on Weteringschans.'

Wout promised to pick it up for me.

The next morning I met Uncle Hannes at the bus stop on Surinameplein. He was an old man with a ruddy, deeply lined, weather-beaten face. I was carrying the suitcase with clothes. I'd left my brother's bag with Wout. I didn't know where we were going and didn't ask. I saw that we had left the city and now found ourselves on a country road with meadows on either side.

At a crossroad, Uncle Hannes signalled me and we got out. The bus took off with a roar. The old man produced a bicycle from behind a tree and tied my suitcase onto the rear luggage rack.

'Walk down this road,' he said, 'until you get to the fifth farm house.' He nodded at me and got on his bike.

I stood at the crossroad and watched him ride away with my suitcase bouncing up and down on the rack. In the distance was a cloud of dust that obscured the bus. It must have been around noon, for the sun was high in the sky. The air shimmered above the fields. I walked in the track left by

Uncle Hannes's bike and felt the sun beating on my head and back. I was glad the old man had taken my suitcase, for it turned out to be a long walk to the fifth farmhouse. When I got there, I saw an old farmer's wife standing in the yard.

'Come on in,' she said.

In a dark, low-ceilinged room a lot of people were sitting at a long table with Uncle Hannes at the head. Someone pulled up a chair for me and set a cup of milk in front of me. The milk was cool. There was a large platter with sandwiches in the middle of the table. Everyone took some. The woman next to me put a couple on my plate.

'You have to eat, dear,' she said, smiling. She had dark hair that she wore in a big knot at the nape of her neck. Her hands were long and slender. They were beautiful hands, with thin fingers and pointed nails, the hands of a woman who on Friday evenings lays the white damask cloth on the table, places the silver Kiddush cup next to the bottle of wine and covers the bread with the embroidered cloth. I thought of my mother, of how she used to set the table on Friday nights and how we would wait in the bright, familiar room for my father to come home from the synagogue. Then we would usher in the Sabbath with a sip of wine and a piece of bread.

'Do eat something,' said the woman next to me.

I picked up a sandwich and looked around the table. There were women wearing brightly coloured aprons and men in overalls. None of them looked like farmers.

A little boy across from me stared at me in curiosity with dark brown eyes while stuffing his chubby cheeks with bread. The woman next to me poured me another cup of milk.

'My daughter is about your age,' she said. She smiled.

'Oh, really?' I said. 'It was hot on the road.'

'It's cool here,' she said. 'I don't know where she is.'

'Who?' I asked.

'My daughter,' she said.

'Oh, right,' I said. Then added, 'I had to walk a long way.'

'It's very remote here,' said the woman. 'She was supposed to have been here too; it would have worked out all right.'

'Oh, yes,' I said, 'it's a long way from the crossroad.'

'Are you going to stay here?' she asked.

'I don't know,' I said.

After the meal, Uncle Hannes clasped his hands together and prayed. The others bowed their heads, then got up after the prayer and left the room. I was the only one left at the table.

'You've seen how many people I have hiding here,' Uncle Hannes said to me.

I nodded. 'I've seen it,' I said.

'I can't shelter you here,' he said. 'You'll have to go somewhere else.'

'All right,' I said.

'The boy will take you,' continued Uncle Hannes. He went over and stood by the window. A girl with red cheeks came and cleared the table.

'Do you see that tree over there?' asked Uncle Hannes. He pointed outside. I got up from the empty table and stood next to him. 'When you reach that tree, you'll see a railway crossing. Wait there for the boy.'

The girl with the red cheeks started sweeping up the straw and breadcrumbs. There were a few crusts under the chair where the boy with the dark brown eyes had been sitting. I walked hesitantly to the door, not knowing if I was supposed to leave right away. Uncle Hannes continued to stare out the window. The girl swept the crumbs into a dustpan.

'Good luck,' said Uncle Hannes. He turned around and nodded at me.

I left the room. My suitcase was in the hall. Outside was the blazing sun and the strong odour of manure. I crossed the yard and walked up the road without looking back.

The bed

The boy came riding up with two bikes. I was waiting for him at the unguarded railway crossing and saw the wind blow a shock of his light blond hair away from his sunburned face. He leaned the bikes against a post, took my suitcase and tied it to his luggage rack.

'We have to go that way,' he said, pointing to a path that ran through a pasture. I nodded and got on my bike. He rode ahead of me over the sandy road. Meanwhile it had got even hotter. A horse was standing near a gate, flicking flies with its tail. Every now and then a grazing cow turned languidly to stare at us. The boy kept biking without looking around. The dry, loose sand of the path made it more and more difficult to keep my balance. I had to pedal hard to avoid skidding, though things went better after we turned onto another road. At last we came to a canal lined with small houses on both sides.

The boy dropped back to bike next to me. 'We're almost there,' he said. He had tied his handkerchief around his neck. Everywhere women were busy cleaning windows and scrubbing the pavements in front of their houses. Children were playing on the strip of grass along the water. A fisherman sat gazing motionlessly at his float. The boy and I got off our bikes in front of one of the houses. My clothes felt as if they were glued to my body.

'This is it,' said the boy. We walked over a gravel path to the back, where an open door led to a kitchen.

A woman was peeling potatoes at the table.

She had a thin face with a narrow pointed nose and stringy blonde hair.

'Here she is,' said the boy.

'Who?' asked the woman, looking up.

'The girl,' said the boy.

'So soon?' She remained sitting, a half-peeled potato in one hand and the other brushing back a strand of hair.

'You knew about it, didn't you?' said the boy. 'You signed up, didn't you?'

'Yes, I did,' said the woman. She spoke with a slight drawl. 'But I didn't know she'd come so soon.'

'Well, she's come now,' said the boy. I was standing halfway in the door, with one foot on the gravel and the other on the threshold. The woman glanced at me, then went on peeling.

'We don't have a bed,' she said.

'Someone will bring you one,' said the boy.

'When?'

'Today, maybe. Or else tomorrow, I think.'

'That better be true,' she said.

'I'm off,' he said, stepping outside and waving his hand. 'Good luck,' he called out to me. And off he went, riding one bike and wheeling the other beside him, just as I'd seen him do when he came to fetch me at the railway crossing.

'Have a seat,' said the woman. I sat down on the other side of the table. One by one the peeled potatoes landed with a splash in the tub, splattering the water against my leg. I shivered each time, but I kept my leg right where it was, waiting for the spray like a person who's dying of thirst and is given a few drops at a time.

'We eat a lot of potatoes,' said the woman when the tub was full.

'I suppose you have a large family?' I asked.

'There are six of us,' she said, 'and another one's on the way.'

'There were five of us,' I said. I couldn't remember so many potatoes being peeled in our house.

'Are all the others gone?' she asked.

'Yes,' I said.

'They say that no one ever comes back from there.' She looked up.

Outside the gravel crunched. A couple of boys ran into the kitchen, followed by a big burly man with huge hands.

He looked at me in silence. The boys also stopped in their tracks when they caught sight of me.

'We don't have a bed,' said the woman.

'Well,' said the man, 'aren't they going to bring us one?'

'The boy said it might come today, or else tomorrow.'

'Oh well,' he said. 'Meanwhile she can share our bed with you and I'll crawl in with the boys.' He sank into an old armchair and put his feet on the edge of the table. He was wearing heavy black socks. He'd removed his wooden shoes and left them by the door.

'We'll tell everyone that you're our niece from Rotterdam,' he said to me.

'We don't have any relatives in Rotterdam,' said the woman.

'Yes, we do,' he said. 'At any rate, I have a nephew who used to live there.'

'What if they don't bring the bed?' the woman started in again.

'Then I'll go get it,' said the man. He rolled a cigarette. The woman threw a stick of wood in the stove and placed the pot of potatoes on top. The wood crackled and smelled of resin and smoke. The children had gone outside. Once in a while they peeked in through the window. A sweltering heat filled the kitchen. The woman set the plates on the table. There were seven plates.

The top

Our neighbour, Rinus, was sitting by the water, fishing. I sat down beside him and looked at his float.

'Would you like to go rowing?' he asked. He sat perfectly still with his fishing rod in his hand and his wooden leg sticking out in front of him on the grass like an abandoned oar.

'Yes,' I said, 'I'd like to go rowing this afternoon.'

'All right,' he said. 'Just take the boat. I don't need it.'

He'd lent me his rowing boat before because he didn't use it very often himself. He could usually be found fishing on the banks of the canal. Ever since he'd lost a leg – in a tractor incident, as he once told me – he didn't do much any more. I lingered for a while longer. The sun warmed my back and made me feel so lethargic that I wished I could have lain by the water all afternoon. But I needed to go to the village.

'Look,' said Rinus, 'there's another one.'

At first I thought he'd caught a fish, but he was looking at a silver speck droning through the blue sky.

'It's not going to last much longer,' he said. 'You'll see.' I was reminded of my father, who had always said the same thing. Rinus looked down again at his float and kept his eyes on the water even when more aeroplanes flew over. I stood up, went over to the boat, pushed it away from the bank and rowed with slow strokes to the middle of the pond while Rinus kept getting farther and farther away. The only sound was the sloshing of the water against the side of the boat. Before I knew what was happening, I'd ended up among the reeds. I pulled the oars into the boat and stayed in my seat. At that moment everything seemed normal. I was rowing on a nice summer afternoon. Off in the distance a train whistled. It was filled with people going on holiday. By peering over the reeds, I could see the greenhouses in Aalsmeer. They were full of flowers – flowers to put in vases, flowers for a birthday. Happy birthday and here's a bouquet! I managed to go rowing this afternoon. Being on the water was glorious. Just then a frog jumped into the reeds with a loud splash. I needed to hurry. I managed to get out from between the reeds and rowed in the direction of the village.

I had agreed to meet Wout in the café by the station. I sat down by the window to wait for him. There were few customers. A record player was blaring out German songs.

Outside children were playing with a top. I saw Wout coming up behind them, with my brother's bag under his arm.

'Are you getting along OK here?' he asked after seating himself across from me. He pulled some books out of the bag.

I nodded. 'Even so, I'd rather be in Amsterdam,' I said.

'Why?' asked Wout. 'Things are relatively quiet here. It's a lot less safe for you in Amsterdam.'

'It's as if I'm on holiday,' I said. 'I row a lot, I lie in the sun, I help a bit around the house – and the rest of the time I do nothing.'

'You wouldn't be able to do anything in Amsterdam either,' he said.

'Have you made any enquiries?' I asked.

'Yes,' he said, looking out the window. 'They've been sent on to the East.'

I followed his gaze.

'It's top season, now,' I said.

A little girl was spinning her top – a red one – on the pavement. She lashed it with a whip, which sent it flying in an elegant arc onto the road, where it twirled around like a ballet dancer, right in front of an oncoming truck.

Wout toyed with a beer coaster, making it tilt sideways, roll across the table then fall on top of his fingers. A few soldiers went by. Their heavy footsteps resounded for a very long time. Meanwhile, the girl had retrieved her squashed top.

'But they'll come back, won't they?' I asked.

'Yes,' said Wout. 'Maybe it'll all be over soon.'

'Let's get out of here,' I said.

We stood up. A German soldier was coming into the café just as I was going out, so that we both went through the revolving door at the same time.

Outside the little girl was crying over her top.

A new name

The bed that Uncle Hannes had promised to bring never arrived and the man didn't go and pick it up. He came home exhausted every evening and got up at the crack of dawn the next day. He was a day labourer at a farm and the work was very heavy, especially in the summer. He took it easy on Sundays and slept most of the day. Occasionally he'd horse around with his wife, but it never lasted long, because she'd soon get annoyed.

All that time the woman and I had to sleep in the same bed while the man slept in the other bed with the boys. It was very stuffy in the low-ceilinged attic, which was never aired. I slept badly, hardly daring to move for fear I would touch the woman. She'd told me she never washed herself.

'After all, I'm not dirty,' she said. 'I change my clothes once a week.'

'I suppose you had a bigger house?' asked the man.

'Yes,' I said.

'And enough beds?' asked the woman.

'Lots,' I said. 'We often had guests.'

'How many?' the woman wanted to know.

I thought about it. I no longer had a clear image of the house. I could picture the street in Breda, the meadow on one side and the front gardens on the other side, the pothole in the road that I always biked across, the sagging kerb where I used to veer onto the pavement, the door hatch that you could push open and reach through to get to the lock. I saw the swinging door that creaked as it fell shut, the hallway, the doors to the rooms. The staircase.

'I forget,' I said.

'Well,' said the woman, 'there must have been enough.'

'I think so,' I said.

'It's such a pity,' she said, 'a house like that.'

'What's such a pity?' asked the man.

'Well,' she said, 'a house like that, with everything in it.'

'When the war is over,' I said, 'I'm certain we'll go and live in it again.'

'Maybe so,' said the man. He looked at me as he rolled a cigarette. 'Maybe so,' he repeated after wetting the cigarette paper with his tongue.

It was the last night I spent with them. I was leaving the next day. The money Dave had left for me in his bag was running out. Now that I could no longer pay, I didn't want to burden this poor family. Wout had found a place for me in Heemstede.

I had seated myself at the kitchen table and was bleaching my hair. The black was beginning to show through again. Thanks to frequent use, the peroxide that had turned my hair light blonde had ceased to hurt.

'It's better to be a natural blonde,' said the woman.

'But she's not,' said the man. 'If she was, she wouldn't be here.'

'You people are always dark, aren't you?' she said.

'No,' I said, 'not always.'

'Anyway, you can always tell what they are,' she said, pensively rubbing her round belly. 'I once knew a Jew,' she said. 'He was a decent man. He often visited the lady I used to work for.'

The following day I met Wout at the bus stop. I saw him looking at my hair.

'Is there something the matter?' I asked.

'No,' he said, 'there's nothing suspicious about you.'

But I wasn't so sure. Although I had become used to the idea of getting caught one day, I still felt ill at ease during the trip.

'Just act normally,' said Wout.

I thought back to the time when I actually *had* been normal and wondered how it had felt. I'd forgotten how I looked when I walked down the street, how I felt when I boarded the train, what I said when I entered a shop. Wout had brought along my new identity card and had given it to me before we'd got into the bus. I'd already thrown away the old one. It had cost a fortune but had been of very poor quality. This one had cost nothing.

'What kind of name have you given me?' I asked him.

'A beautiful name,' he replied.

I couldn't help thinking of one of my aunts, who had once been seriously ill. They had prayed for her in the synagogue and had given her another name – a beautiful name taken from the Bible – and she had recovered.

In the bus I inspected the identity card. It had a photo of me with my light hair, as well as a fingerprint. I read the name. It felt as though I was being introduced to myself. I repeated the name a few times, softly to myself.

Later, when we were walking past a narrow waterway, Wout pointed to a low, old house.

'This is it,' he said. 'You'll be completely safe here.'

We crossed a bridge with an iron railing. A tall blonde girl came toward us. I told her my name – my new name.

Epilogue

The tram stop

Some weeks after liberation, I went to visit my uncle in Zeist. The Germans had left him alone because he was married to a non-Jewish woman. Although I hadn't written to let him know I was coming, I saw him standing at the tram stop.

'How did you know that I'd be here?' I asked him.

'I wait here every day,' he said, 'to see if your father is coming.'

'But you got a message from the Red Cross, didn't you?' I asked.

'Yes, I did,' he said. 'They now say that he won't be coming back, but I don't believe it. You can never know for sure, can you?'

We crossed the square and walked to his house, which was only a minute or two away. I hadn't seen my uncle in years and found him quite changed. He must have been in his fifties, but he shuffled wearily beside me like a person who no longer expects anything from life. His hair had turned white, his face was yellow, and his cheeks were hollow. Though he had always looked a lot like my father, I could no longer see a resemblance. He was not the jolly, carefree uncle he used to be. He paused in front of the door of his house.

'Don't mention any of this to your aunt,' he said, bending closer to me. 'She just doesn't understand.'

He inserted the key in the lock. I followed him up the stairs to a small, gloomy room where my aunt was pouring tea. My uncle seated himself in an armchair by the window.

'You can see the tram arrive from here,' he said, 'which is very convenient. There's now a regular service to Utrecht again.' He got up and shuffled out of the room.

'Your uncle is ill,' my aunt informed me. 'Fortunately, he doesn't know it, but he's not ever going to get well. The news about the family really hit him hard.'

I nodded. I said that I could tell and that I found him quite changed.

'Shh,' she said, putting her finger to her lips. He came back in.

'Look,' said my uncle, pointing to a couple of dark garments that he was carrying over his arm. 'This is a nice suit. There's absolutely nothing wrong with it.'

'Is it yours?' I asked.

'I've been saving it all these years,' he said. 'It was hanging in the wardrobe with mothballs.' There was a note of triumph in his voice when he whispered to me, 'For your father!'

Carefully he hung the suit over a chair and continued, 'I've also got a pair of shoes in the wardrobe. As good as new. Would you like to see them?'

'Later perhaps,' I said. But he forgot about it, for when I got up to leave shortly afterwards, he quickly threw on his coat.

'I'll go with you,' he said, checking his watch. 'The tram is due to arrive any minute.'

Instead the tram was just about to leave. I said goodbye hurriedly and jumped in. From the rear platform I waved to him as the tram pulled away. But he didn't wave back. He was looking at the tram coming from the opposite direction, which I realised was the one he'd meant. Before we rounded the bend, I saw him, small and stooped, peering at the passengers getting off the tram. Later on, I went to see him several times without giving him any advance notice and I always found him waiting at the tram stop. With every visit he looked older and sicker and showed me the suit he'd been saving in his wardrobe.

One day I received word from my aunt that my uncle had died. I went back to Zeist and, in the tram, I thought how strange it would be not to see my uncle at the stop. I automatically looked for him when I got out.

In the half-darkened room my aunt was sitting at the table, working on a crossword puzzle with a finely sharpened pencil in her hand. I sat down in the chair by the window and pushed the curtain back a bit. I could see part of the tram shelter at the end of the street.

'He really liked to sit there,' said my aunt. 'He used to watch for the tram.'

'You can see it coming from here,' I said.

'Yes,' she said, 'he used to say that too. I've actually never seen it clearly.' She came over to stand by me and bent down. 'Barely,' she said, 'you can barely see it.'

But that wasn't true. From my uncle's chair the stop was clearly visible. At last I understood why my uncle had told me not to discuss it with my aunt. Just before I left, she came in carrying the suit.

'Here,' she said. 'Your uncle told me to give it to you.'

'It's of no use to me,' I said. 'Please give it to someone who can put it to good use.' As I was leaving the room, my aunt bent back over her crossword puzzle. I slowly made my way to the tram stop. I had already noticed that there was no tram waiting, but meanwhile one had arrived from the opposite direction.

I stopped to look at the people getting out, as if I were waiting for someone. Someone with a familiar face who would suddenly be standing right in front of me. But I lacked my uncle's faith. They would never come back. Not my father, not my mother, not Bettie, not Dave and not Lotte, either.

Translator's note

Bitter Herbs was first published in 1957, and the next year Marga Minco was awarded the Vijverberg Prize of the Jan Campert Foundation for the best Dutch debut novel. It was incredibly well received and made the author into one of the best known Dutch writers of the post-war era. *Bitter Herbs* eventually became required high school reading in the Netherlands. In her acceptance speech at the Vijverberg Prize ceremony, Minco said:

> 'I would have preferred not to have had a reason to write *Bitter Herbs*. But the facts are there, as is the book. And what counts for me is that those to whom I dedicated the book will now perhaps live on, and not only in my memory.'

In the twenty-two chapters of *Bitter Herbs* the narrator recounts what happened to her family during World War II.

The story parallels events in the author's life but is not strictly autobiographical since the narrator is a girl between 14 and 18 years old while the author was between 20 and 25 when the events of *Bitter Herbs* took place. The narrator should therefore not be confused with the author. The girl's innocence and ignorance illustrate the unawareness and incomprehension of most Dutch Jews about the lot awaiting them.

The chapters were written at different times as individual stories, and so can be read separately, but in the end Minco arranged them in chronological order and added to them to create *Bitter Herbs*. The chapter *Lepelstraat* is an example. In 1943, when she lived in Sarphatistraat with her parents, the author witnessed the forced removal of the residents of Lepelstraat in the heart of the Jewish area of Amsterdam. Minco wrote about the event, but she lost her writings and many other things after her escape. However, when she was organising and arranging the stories, she remembered what she had witnessed in Lepelstraat and managed to rewrite it almost word for word. In 1948 or 1949 she wrote *The garden gate,* later retitled *The men,* which became a key chapter of *Bitter Herbs.* The chapter *Camping mugs* was published as a standalone piece in a literary magazine in 1953.

Minco's style is deceptively simple, beautiful, and direct. In translating her work, there are times that an extra word or two had to be added in order for twenty-first-century readers to understand references that would have been obvious to readers in the post-World War II era. And not only that – there is a difference between the Dutch for whom World War II is still an ever-present reality, and the rest of the world.

Unavoidably there are many Dutch place names in the book, and mostly it's clear that those are streets and squares in Amsterdam and in other Dutch cities. But in the chapter *Bitter herbs*, the narrator wants to see her parents again before they're deported and says to her brother: 'I could wait in front of the Hollandse Schouwburg where they're being held.' The Hollandse Schouwburg [Dutch Theatre] has a significance that may not be immediately obvious. Before the war it was a theatre, but during the occupation, the Germans made it into a Jewish theatre where only Jews could perform and only Jews were allowed in the audience. Starting in mid-October 1942, it was turned into the central deportation centre where the Germans processed the Jews for removal from Amsterdam to transit camps Westerbork and Vught (and from there to the East: Auschwitz, Sobibor, etc.). Enormous crowds were interned in the theatre, at times more than 1,500 people with their allowed baggage. They were stuck there for days and sometimes weeks with no room to sleep, abominable hygienic conditions and unbearable noise. In 1962 it was made into a national memorial to the deported Jews.

Jeannette K. Ringold

About the author

Marga Minco is a Dutch writer who was born in 1920. She debuted as an author in 1957 with *Bitter Herbs*, which was followed by other famous works such as *An Empty House* (1966), *The Fall* (1983) and many short stories. She won the Vijverberg prize in 1957, the Annie Romein Prize in 1999, the Constantijn Huygen Prize in 2005 and the P.C. Hooft Prize in 2019 for her entire oeuvre.

About the translator

Jeannette K. Ringold has translated more than 20 fiction and non-fiction works by Dutch authors into English. She was born in the Netherlands and now lives in California.